Dear Parent:

Congratulations! Your child is taking the first steps on an exciting journey. The destination? Independent reading!

STEP INTO READING® will help your child get there. The program offers five steps to reading success. Each step includes fun stories and colorful art. There are also Step into Reading Sticker Books, Step into Reading Math Readers, Step into Reading Phonics Readers, Step into Reading Write-In Readers, and Step into Reading Phonics Boxed Sets—a complete literacy program with something for every child.

Learning to Read, Step by Step!

Ready to Read Preschool–Kindergarten
• big type and easy words • rhyme and rhythm • picture clues
For children who know the alphabet and are eager to begin reading.

Reading with Help Preschool–Grade 1
• basic vocabulary • short sentences • simple stories
For children who recognize familiar words and sound out new words with help.

Reading on Your Own Grades 1–3
• engaging characters • easy-to-follow plots • popular topics
For children who are ready to read on their own.

Reading Paragraphs Grades 2–3
• challenging vocabulary • short paragraphs • exciting stories
For newly independent readers who read simple sentences with confidence.

Ready for Chapters Grades 2–4
• chapters • longer paragraphs • full-color art
For children who want to take the plunge into chapter books but still like colorful pictures.

STEP INTO READING® is designed to give every child a successful reading experience. The grade levels are only guides. Children can progress through the steps at their own speed, developing confidence in their reading, no matter what their grade.

Remember, a lifetime love of reading starts with a single step!

For little heroes everywhere!
—B. W.

RHUS27216

All rights reserved. Published in the United States by Random House Children's Books, a division of Random House, Inc., 1745 Broadway, New York, NY 10019, and in Canada by Random House of Canada Limited, Toronto.

Step into Reading, Random House, and the Random House colophon are registered trademarks of Random House, Inc.

Visit us on the Web!
StepIntoReading.com
randomhouse.com/kids
dckids.kidswb.com

Educators and librarians, for a variety of teaching tools, visit us at RHTeachersLibrarians.com

ISBN 978-0-307-98119-6 (trade) – ISBN 978-0-307-98120-2 (lib. bdg.) –
ISBN 978-0-307-98121-9 (ebook)
Printed in the United States of America
10 9 8 7 6 5 4 3 2 1

STEP INTO READING®

STEP 2

DC★SUPER FRIENDS™

BIZARRO DAY!

By Billy Wrecks

Illustrated by Francesco Legramandi

Random House 🏠 New York

Bizarro lives on
a strange planet
called Bizarro World.

Bizarro wants to be like his hero, Superman.

But Bizarro is
Superman's opposite.
He always gets
things wrong.

The <u>S</u> on Bizarro's chest
is reversed.

Superman flies
straight and fast.

But Bizarro flies
crooked and slow.

Superman's heat vision
can cut through anything.

Bizarro has freeze vision.

BRRRR!

Superman's super-breath
cools off hot volcanoes.

But watch out:

Bizarro breathes fire!

Bizarro sees Earth.

He has an idea!

He will visit

the Super Friends.

They will show him

how to be a hero!

Bizarro lands
in Metropolis.
CRUNCH!
He stops the Penguin.

"Bizarro wants to be
a hero," he says.
"Me make good start!"
(Bizarro talks funny, too.)

The Super Friends
will teach Bizarro.

Batman is quiet
when catching the
bad guys.

But Bizarro is loud!

The Flash is fast
when stopping
the bad guys.

Bizarro is slow—
but he still stops
the bad guys!

Green Lantern
always helps
people in need.

Bizarro tries to help.

But he makes mistakes.

Bizarro flies off
to find Superman.
The Super Friends
follow him.

Lex Luthor has
Superman.
He is chained up
with Kryptonite.

The green rock
makes Superman weak.
Bizarro races to help.

Bizarro breaks the chains,
takes the Kryptonite . . .

. . . and throws it
far into space!

Superman is saved!
He makes a gift
for Bizarro.

"You may be different," Superman says, "but today you are <u>my</u> hero."

Bizarro heads home.

He is happy because

he is a real hero!